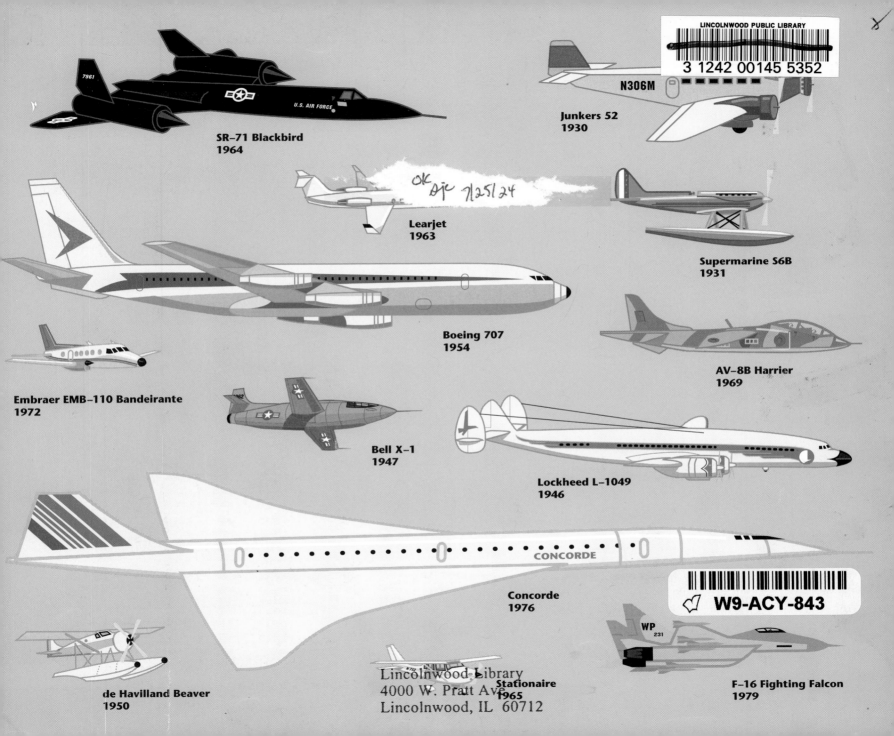

SR–71 Blackbird
1964

Junkers 52
1930

N306M

OK
djc 7/25/24

Learjet
1963

Supermarine S6B
1931

Boeing 707
1954

Embraer EMB–110 Bandeirante
1972

AV–8B Harrier
1969

Bell X–1
1947

Lockheed L–1049
1946

Concorde
1976

de Havilland Beaver
1950

Stationaire
1965

F–16 Fighting Falcon
1979

TAKE OFF!

by Ryan Ann Hunter
illustrated by Edward Miller

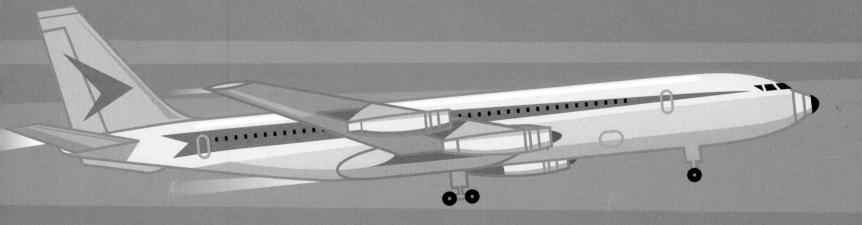

Holiday House / New York

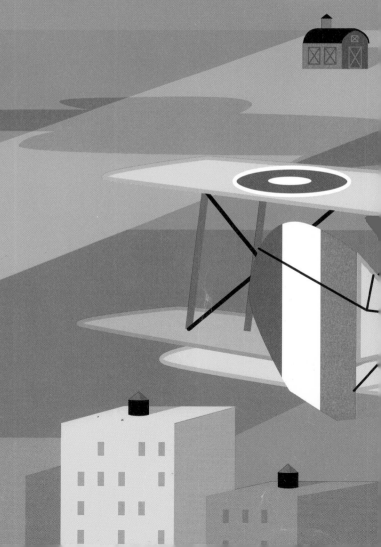

For our editor, Mary Cash, who helps our
words take flight—E. G. M. and P. D. G.

To my sister, Lorrie—E. M.

Library of Congress Cataloging-in-Publication Data
Hunter, Ryan Ann.
    Take off! / by Ryan Ann Hunter; illustrated by Edward Miller.—1st ed.
        p.   cm.
    Summary: Surveys the history, achievements, activities, and technology of aviation.
    ISBN 0-8234-1466-3
1. Aeronautics—Juvenile literature. [1. Aeronautics.]
I. Miller, Ed. 1964- ill. II. Title
TL547.H815 1999
629.13—DC21   98-45423   CIP   AC

The authors would like to thank Dennis Parks at
the Museum of Flight in Seattle, Gordon Yano
at Lawrence Livermore Laboratory, and
John Baldwin, pilot, for their assistance.

Airplanes take you off the ground, up over houses and barns and skyscrapers.

Monk Eilmer
1060

Otto Lilienthal
1891–1896

Marquis d'Arlandes and
Jean-Francois Pilâtre de Rozier
1783

People have always wanted to fly. Long before they understood
how, they told stories about winged shoes, and winged horses,
and magic carpets. People tried flapping huge, homemade wings.
But they couldn't stay up in the air at all.

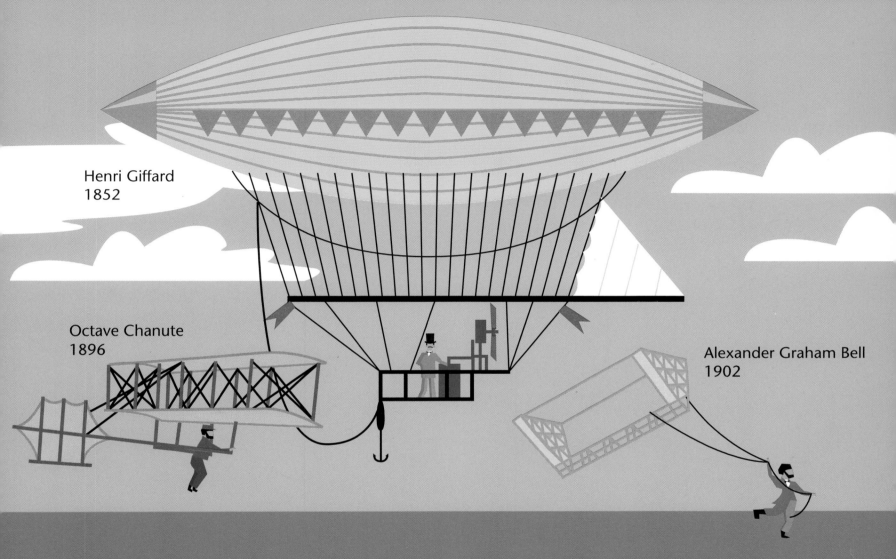

Henri Giffard
1852

Octave Chanute
1896

Alexander Graham Bell
1902

Then they thought of floating. They got off the ground in a hot air balloon. But they could only go where the wind took them. People kept studying birds and gliders and kites. Finally, they figured it out.

If a plane has the right wings, if it is strong and light, and if it goes fast enough, it flies.

On December 17, 1903, the Wright brothers tested their plane, **Flyer**. Orville lay flat on the bottom wing. He flew 120 feet. He and Wilbur took turns. Finally, Wilbur flew 852 feet.

Soon more and more people were flying.

Many early planes were biplanes. They had double-layer wings and open cockpits. Flying was cold and noisy and windy. But people didn't mind. They entered all kinds of races. Who could fly the highest? The fastest? Who could be first to cross the English Channel?

Louis Bleriot
July 25, 1909
(*first to cross the English Channel*)

Curtiss JN–4H
1918

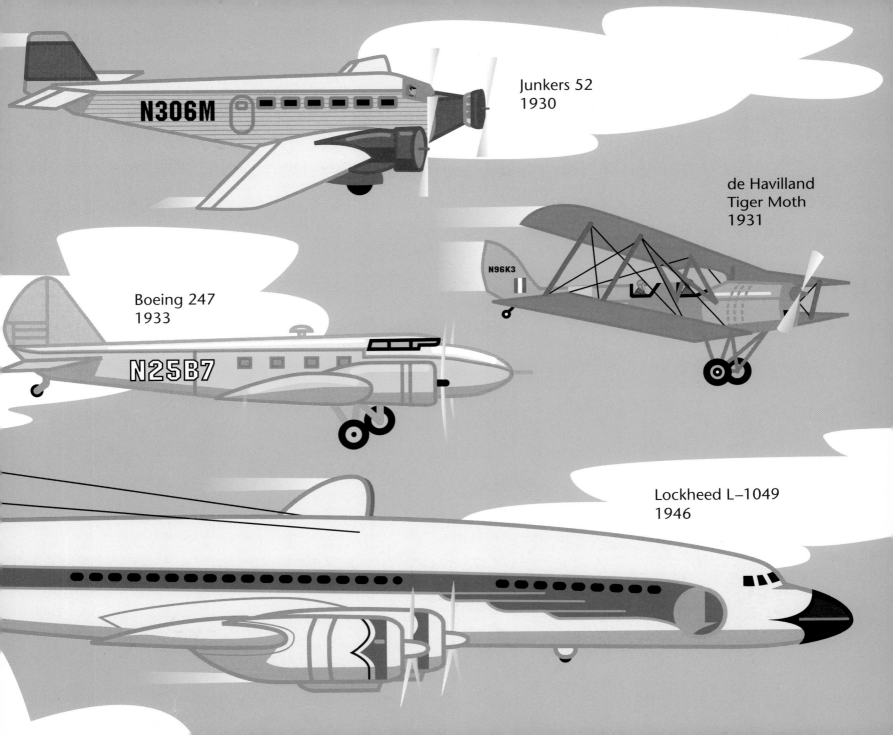

Junkers 52
1930

de Havilland
Tiger Moth
1931

Boeing 247
1933

Lockheed L–1049
1946

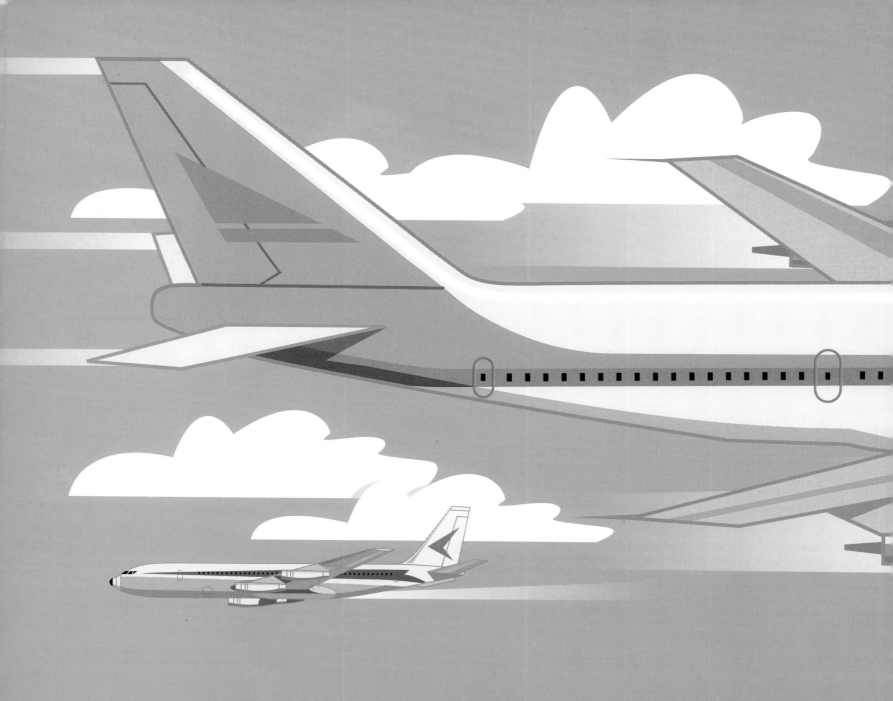

Now planes fly even higher and faster and farther. They are streamlined, with swept-back wings and jet engines.

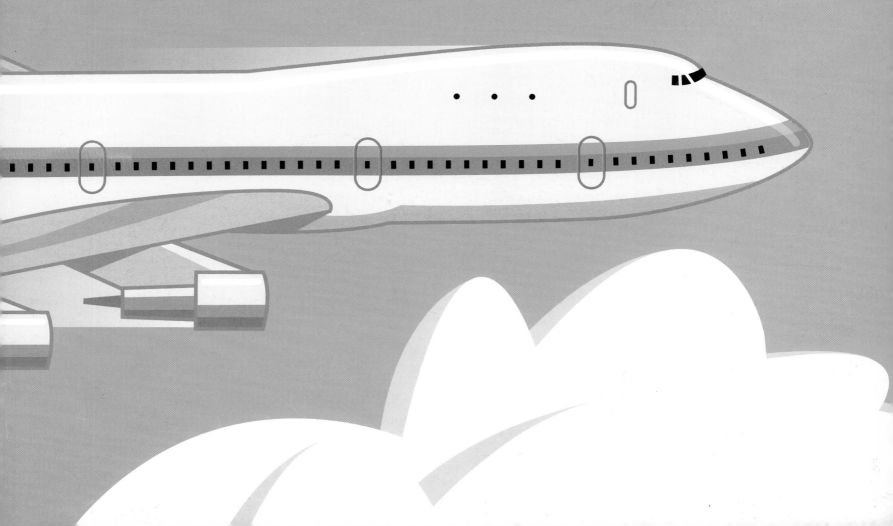

Today, all kinds of airplanes do all kinds of work.

Sky Writing

Transporting Freight

Fire Fighting

Carrying Commuters

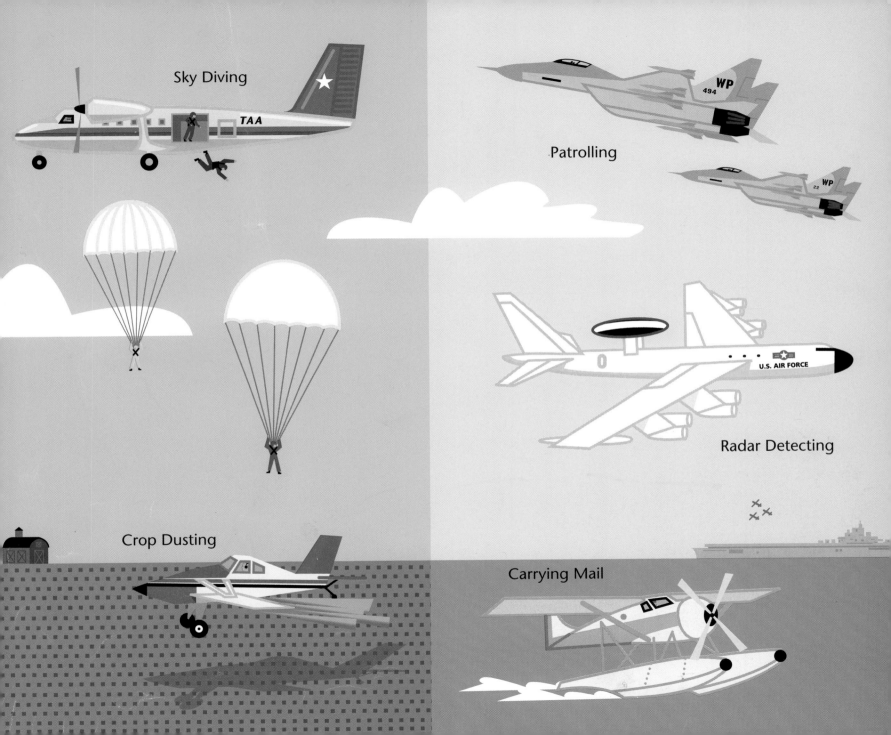

Sky Diving

Patrolling

Radar Detecting

Crop Dusting

Carrying Mail

Airports are busy. Keeping things running smoothly is a big job. Controllers watch moving blips on radar screens. They talk over radios to guide the pilots.

"Alaska one-two-zero, you are clear to taxi to runway three-six."

TO RW 36

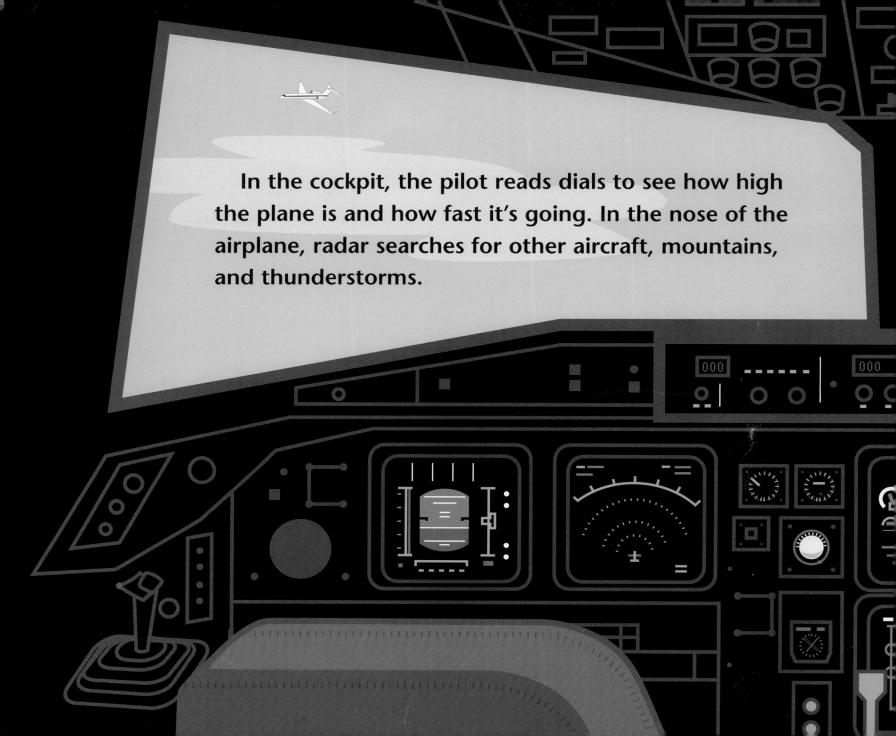

In the cockpit, the pilot reads dials to see how high the plane is and how fast it's going. In the nose of the airplane, radar searches for other aircraft, mountains, and thunderstorms.

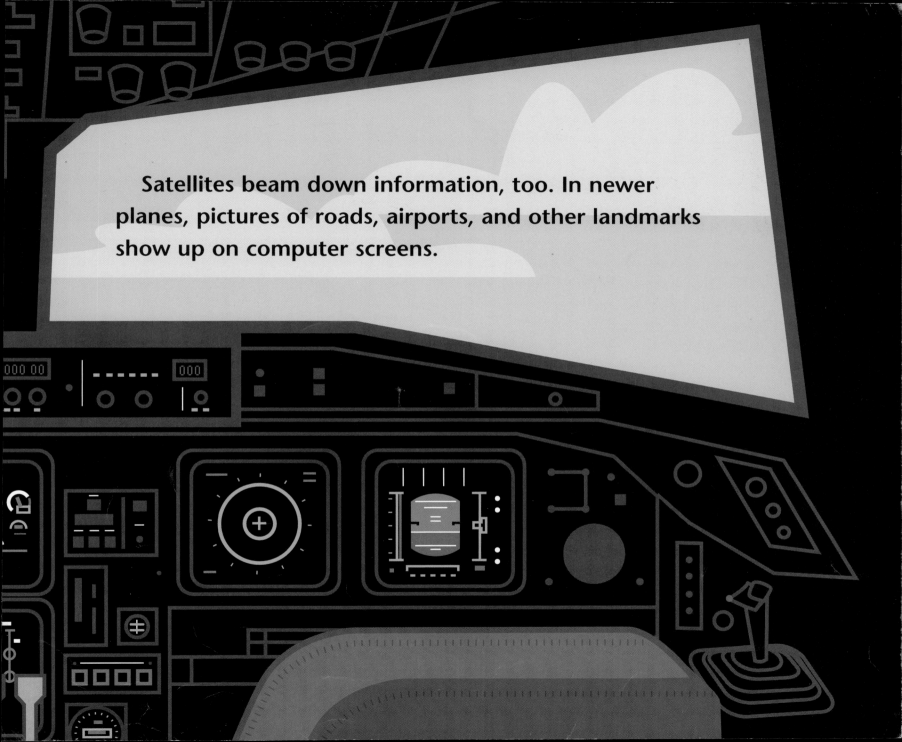

Satellites beam down information, too. In newer planes, pictures of roads, airports, and other landmarks show up on computer screens.

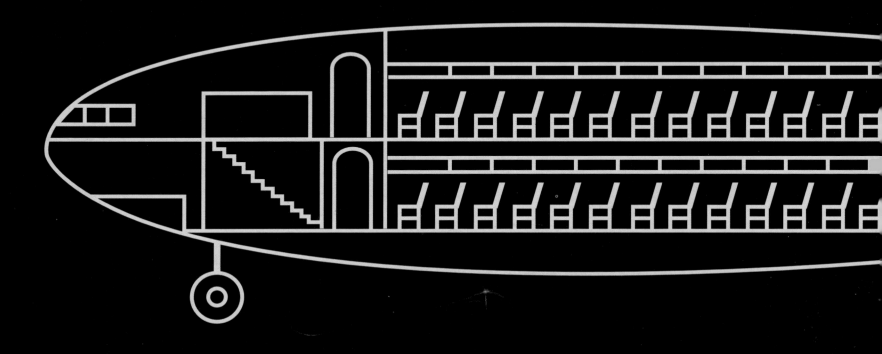

Engineers are always testing new designs. Some want to build megaplanes that could seat 1,000 people in double decks. That would mean fewer planes at busy airports and fewer traffic jams in the air.

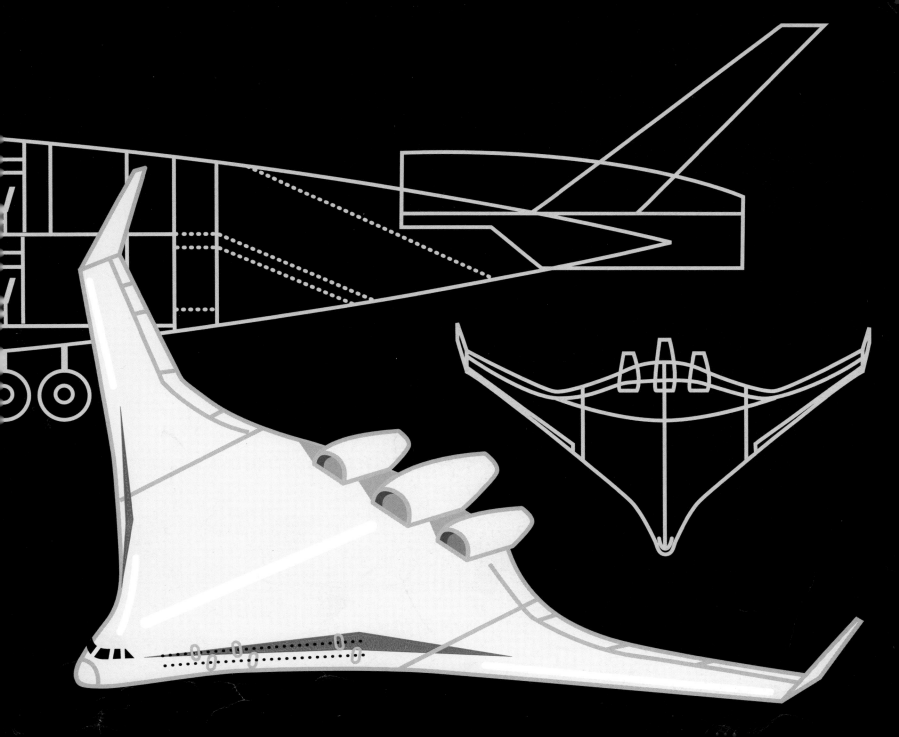

People keep wanting to go faster than ever before. On October 14, 1947, Chuck Yeager used rocket power to fly faster than Mach 1: the speed of sound.

Now the supersonic **Concorde** flies from New York to Paris at Mach 2.

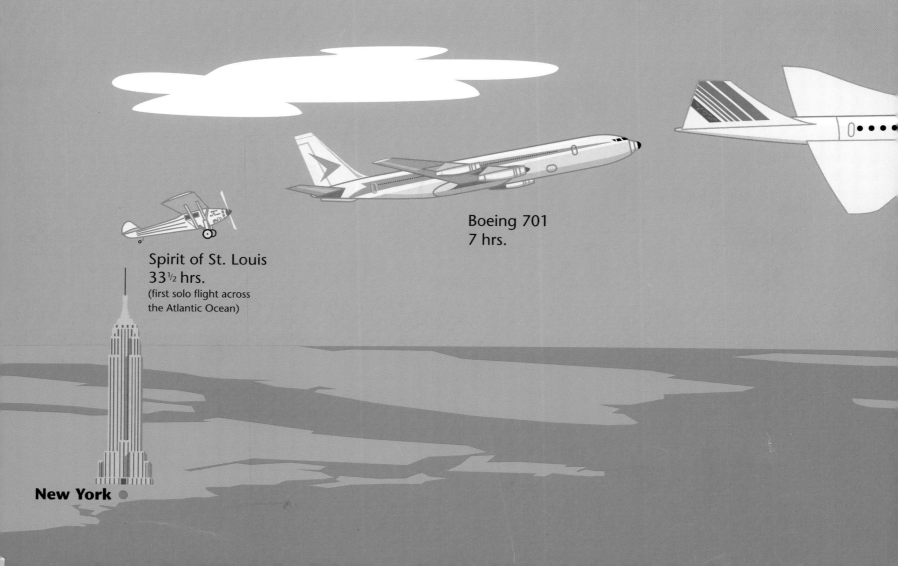

Spirit of St. Louis
33½ hrs.
(first solo flight across the Atlantic Ocean)

Boeing 701
7 hrs.

New York

The **Blackbird** spy plane has gone even faster than that.

Concorde
3 hrs.

SR–71 Blackbird
2 hrs.

Paris

And someday, aerospace planes will go faster
than Mach 10, more than 40 miles above the earth.
Are you ready to fly on the edge of space?

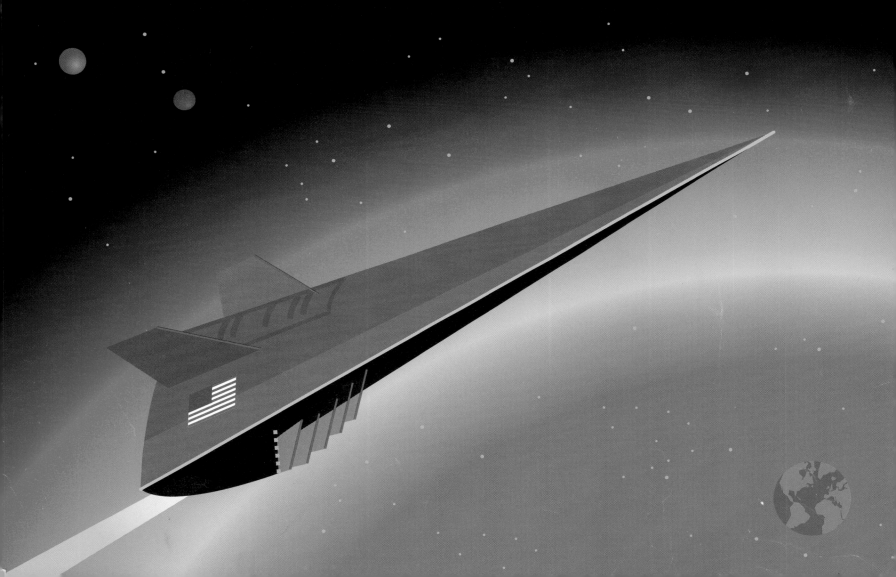

AIRPLANE WINGS

straight wings   **swept-back wings**   **delta wings**

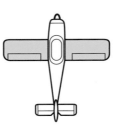  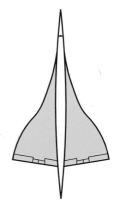

Airplane wings have many different shapes.
Most airplanes with **straight wings** fly at low speeds.
Those with **swept-back wings** can go faster.
Delta wings are used on the fastest planes of all.

Turn back to the picture of planes flying from New York to Paris.
What do the different wing shapes tell you about the speed of each?
Look at the different wing shapes on the endpapers, too.

You can make a paper airplane with **swept-back wings**.
You will need an 8½" x 11" piece of paper and scissors.

1. Fold the paper in half lengthwise.
2. Fold down the front on each side to
 make the nose of the plane.
3. Now fold down the top edge on each
 side to make wings.
4. Cut as shown.
5. Draw in the pilot and passengers on one
 side of the plane, the copilot and more
 passengers on the other, if you like. Add
 your own markings and numbers, too.

How far does your plane fly?
Try making the cuts and folds in different
 places on other planes.
How far do these planes fly?

1.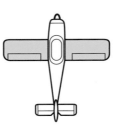

2.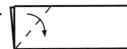

3.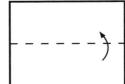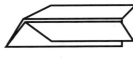

4.

3"   1½"

5.

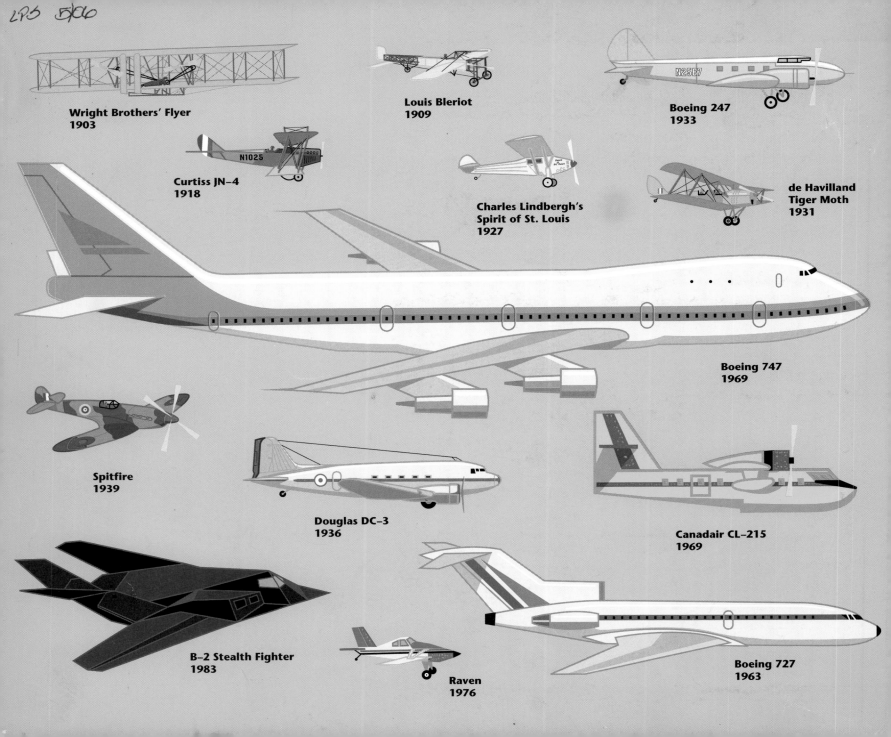

LPS 5/06

Wright Brothers' Flyer
1903

Louis Bleriot
1909

Boeing 247
1933

Curtiss JN-4
1918

**Charles Lindbergh's
Spirit of St. Louis**
1927

**de Havilland
Tiger Moth**
1931

Boeing 747
1969

Spitfire
1939

Douglas DC-3
1936

Canadair CL-215
1969

B-2 Stealth Fighter
1983

Raven
1976

Boeing 727
1963